P9-AFV-280

THIS BOOK IS A GIFT FROM THE
FRIENDS OF THE PINOLE LIBRARY

I AM READING

Miss Wire's Christmas Surprise

IAN WHYBROW

ILLUSTRATED BY

EMMA CHICHESTER CLARK

KINGFISHER

BOSTON

KINGFISHER
a Houghton Mifflin Company imprint
222 Berkeley Street
Boston, Massachusetts 02116
www.houghtonmifflinbooks.com

First published in 1996
2 4 6 8 10 9 7 5 3 1

Text copyright © Ian Whybrow 1996
Illustrations copyright © Emma Chichester Clark 1996

All rights reserved under International and
Pan-American Copyright Conventions

LIBRARY OF CONGRESS CATALOGING-IN-PUBLICATION DATA
has been applied for.

ISBN 978-0-7534-6136-5

Printed in China
1TR/0507/WKT/ - (SC)/115MA/F

Contents

Chapter One
4

Chapter Two
14

Chapter Three
19

Chapter Four
26

Chapter Five
37

Chapter One

This is Miss Wire.

She was old,

but she was full of life.

She had a little bird.

He was full of life too.

Miss Wire was short,

but her full name was very, very long.

Her full name was

Miss Julia Johnson

Dickson Thompson

Annie Maria Wire.

Miss Wire lived with her friends at
the Hideaway Home
in Over the Hill,
near Faraway.

Most of Miss Wire's friends
were sleepy all the time.

They slept in their beds,

in their armchairs,

at the table,

and in front of the TV.

But not Miss Wire . . .

7

Miss Wire liked
to stay wide awake.

She wanted to have fun.

"Tonight is Christmas Eve!" she called.

"Wake up! Put up your stockings!"

8

"Oh, ha-ha, Julia," said the old people.

"Very funny!

Christmas is not for old people.

Christmas is just for children!"

"That's right!" said the nurse.
"Santa is much too busy
to worry about old people at Christmas!"
The nurse looked very wise
in her clean white collar
and her clean white cuffs
and her very, very
stiff white apron.
And she clapped
her clean white hands.
"Bedtime, everyone!"
she said.

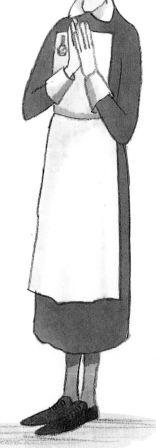

"That means you, Miss Wire."

Clap, clap, clap.

But Miss Wire didn't go to bed.

The Hideaway Home,
Over the Hill,
Faraway.

Christmas Eve,
at 10 o'clock.

Dear Santa,
Sorry to bother you;
My friends are very, very old.
They think that
CHRISTMAS IS NOT FOR OLD PEOPLE.
Can you help?
I hope I am not too late.
I am sending this by small bird.

Love from
Julia Johnson Dickson
Thompson Annie Maria
Wire (aged 95)

Miss Wire wrote a letter.

And this is the letter

that Miss Wire wrote.

12

The little bird

took the letter in his beak

and flew as fast as he could

to the North Pole. Meanwhile . . .

13

Chapter Two

These are three little Christmas Mice.

They came sailing in

on three ships

on Christmas day in the morning.

The three Christmas Mice

were full of life.

They called for their friends

at many a mouse hole.

Most little mice
were having a long winter sleep.
They slept in their nests
all squeezed up together.

But not the Christmas Mice . . .

They liked

to stay wide awake.

They wanted to have fun.

They threw snowballs,

and that was a lot of fun.

They slid on the ice,

and that was a lot of fun.

They made a snow mouse,

and that was a lot of fun.

"But it's Christmas morning!" they said.
"It would be much more fun
to help Santa Claus!"
And they ran to find
a telephone.

Chapter Three

When the telephone rang,
Santa was sitting on his bed,
wearing his red striped pajamas,
reading Miss Wire's letter.

"Hello," said Santa.

"Hello, Santa. Do you need any help?"

asked the Christmas Mice.

"How kind! Help is just what I need,"

said Santa.

"A little bird came to me

this Christmas morning

with a letter.

It is from Miss Julia Johnson

Dickson Thompson

Annie Maria Wire (aged 95).

She sounds very sad.

She says that her old friends

did not put up their stockings.

They think Christmas is just for children."

21

"Are there any presents left?"

asked the Christmas Mice.

"There are some bright balloons,

but nothing else," said Santa. "Except . . ."

"Except what?" said the Christmas Mice.

"Except the Unwanted Toys," said Santa.

"The Unwanted Toys?

Why are they unwanted?"

asked the Christmas Mice.

"People say that they are dangerous,"

said Santa. "They hide in the Dark Places,

afraid that they will harm the children."

"We know the Dark Places,"
said the Christmas Mice.
"We will find these Unwanted Toys
and show the old people
that Christmas is not just for children."
"My reindeer are tired," said Santa.
"Too tired to deliver the Unwanted Toys.
So who will deliver them?"

"Don't worry.

Just ask Miss Wire's little bird

to bring us the balloons,"

said the Christmas Mice.

"And hurry!"

Chapter Four

This is the closet

in a Dark, Dark Place.

The dust lay on the top as thick as tar.

Under the dust there was a cardboard box.

And in the box was a model racecar.

It had sharp pieces sticking out all over.

The mice tapped twice upon the dusty box.

The car said,

"Leave me in this dark, dark room!"

"Somebody wants you,"

said the Christmas Mice.

"So hurry, racer,

you were born to brrrrrrm!"

The little bird tied
a big yellow balloon
to the car, and it flew
out the window.

This is the shed where no one ever went.

High on a shelf and hidden at the back,

behind some cans and jars,

there was a chest.

And in the chest there was

a tin duck that went quack.

He had little flat feet

that went up and down.

"Come on!" the mice said,

lifting up the lid.

"Somebody needs you.

We must go to him."

"No!" sobbed the duck.

"What if I get rusty?"

"Don't cry," the mice said.

"You were born to swim!"

The little bird tied on
a big red balloon,
and the duck
flew out the window.

This is the toy store
where they kept the trunk.

Look what it said:

UNWANTED
DANGEROUS

"Merry Christmas!"

said the Christmas Mice.

"You are all wanted.

Will you come with us?"

And one by one

out crept the DANGEROUS toys.

The stuffed animals said,

"What if the babies swallow our eyes!"

The trains said,

"What if our wheels come off?"

The tin planes said,

"Small children will cut their hands on us!"

The toy soldiers said,

"Little boys will put us in their mouths!"

The glass marbles and the china dolls

were afraid that they might break.

"Watch out! Watch out!"

said the BB guns.

"Watch out for your eyes!"

cried the bows and arrows, the swords,

the pocketknives, and the cannonballs.

"Watch out for your fingers!"

said the toolbox

and the building sets and chemistry sets.

"Don't worry!" said the Christmas Mice.

"We know a place where every toy here

will bring nothing but happiness."

And soon all of the Unwanted Toys
were flying over the hills to Faraway.
The little bird and the Christmas Mice
followed close behind.

Chapter Five

On Christmas morning

at the Hideaway Home

—suddenly!—

all of the beds were full of stuffed animals.

All of the bathtubs were full

of ducks and boats

and swimming frogs!

All of the carpets were covered

with racecars and trains!

And saws were sawing at table legs

and BB guns went pop

and arrows flew

and sword fighters went

one-two, one-two

and dolls were dressed

and then undressed

and growly teddy bears

got their bellies pressed

and marbles got flicked

and went ting and tang

and chemistry sets went

WHIFF! and BANG!

And all of the old people said,
"These toys are *just*
what we always wanted!
Who can we thank
for our best Christmas *ever*?"
"Well," said Miss Wire,
"my little bird tells me
that you should thank
the Christmas Mice."
"Three cheers and thanks
to the Christmas Mice!"
cried the old people.
"And three cheers and thanks
to Miss Wire,"
cried the nurse.

"For she has taught me
that Christmas is not just for children.
Christmas is for *everyone.*"
And the nurse pulled off
her clean white collar
and her clean white cuffs
and her very, very
stiff white apron.

"Come on, everyone," she cried.

"Let's play pirates!"

And everyone joined in.

The little bird joined in.

So did the Christmas Mice

and the old people.

And so did Miss Julia Johnson

Dickson Thompson

Annie Maria Wire (aged 95).

They all had a holly, jolly,

rough, tough time.

And as for the Unwanted Toys,

they were never unwanted again.

About the author and illustrator

Ian Whybrow is the author of the *Shrinky Kid Stories* and of *Quacky quack-quack!*, which was short-listed for the Smarties Award. He says, "I really like the idea of old people playing with toys that are too dangerous for small children. We all need toys, no matter what age we are!"

Emma Chichester Clark won the Mother Goose Award with her first book and is now one of the most popular children's book illustrators. "I enjoyed drawing Miss Wire," says Emma. "She has a lot of spirit—I hope I'm like her when I'm 95."

Strategies for Independent Readers

Predict
Think about the cover, illustrations, and the title
of the book. What do you think this book will be about?
While you are reading think about what may
happen next and why.

Monitor
As you read ask yourself if what you're
reading makes sense. If it doesn't, reread, look
at the illustrations, or read ahead.

Question
Ask yourself questions about important ideas
in the story such as what the characters might
do or what you might learn.

Phonics
If there is a word that you do not know, look carefully
at the letters, sounds, and word parts that you do know.
Blend the sounds to read the word. Ask yourself if this is
a word you know. Does it make sense in the sentence?

Summarize
Think about the characters, the setting where the
story takes place, and the problem the characters faced
in the story. Tell the important ideas in the beginning,
middle, and end of the story.

Evaluate
Ask yourself questions like: Did you like the story?
Why or why not? How did the author make the story
come alive? How did the author make the story fun to
read? How well did you understand the story? Maybe
you can understand it better if you read it again!

3 1901 04999 2896